P9-DMV-341

TO-STAY-BOUND BOOKS
JACKSONVILLE ILLINOIS

MADELINE

story & pictures by

Ludwig Bemelmans

PUFFIN BOOKS

PUFFIN BOOKS
Published by the Penguin Group
Viking Penguin Inc., 40 West 23rd Street, New York, New York 10010, U.S.A.
Penguin Books Ltd, 27 Wrights Lane, London W8 5TZ England
Penguin Books Australia Ltd, Ringwood, Victoria, Australia
Penguin Books Canada Ltd, 2801 John Street, Markham, Ontario, Canada L3R 1B4
Penguin Books (N.Z.) Ltd, 182-190 Wairau Road, Auckland 10, New Zealand

Penguin Books Ltd, Registered Offices: Harmondsworth, Middlesex, England

First published by Simon and Schuster 1939
First published by The Viking Press 1958
Viking Seafarer Edition published 1969
Reprinted 1971, 1972, 1973, 1974, 1975
Published in Picture Puffins 1977
Reprinted 1978 (twice), 1980, 1981, 1982, 1983, 1984 (twice), 1985, 1986, 1987, 1988

Library of Congress Cataloging in Publication Data
Bemelmans, Ludwig. Madeline
Summary: Madeline, smallest and naughtiest of the twelve little charges
of Miss Clavel, wakes up one night with an attack of appendicitis.
[1. France–Fiction. 2. Sick–Fiction. 3. Stories in rhyme] I. Title
[PZ8.3.B425Mag8] [E] 76-50664
ISBN 0 14 050.198 3

Manufactured in the U.S.A.
by Lake Book/Cuneo, Inc., Melrose Park, IL.

Set in Century Expanded

In an old house in Paris

that was covered with vines

lived twelve little girls in two straight lines.

In two straight lines they broke their bread

and brushed their teeth

and went to bed.

They smiled at the good

and frowned at the bad

and sometimes they were very sad.

They left the house
at half past nine
in two straight lines

in rain

or shine—

the smallest one was Madeline.

She was not afraid of mice—

she loved winter, snow, and ice.

To the tiger in the zoo

Madeline just said, "Pooh-pooh,"

and nobody knew so well

how to frighten Miss Clavel.

In the middle of one night

Miss Clavel turned on her light

and said, "Something is not right!"

Little Madeline sat in bed,

cried and cried—her eyes were red.

And soon after Dr. Cohn
came, he rushed out to the phone,

and he dialed: DANton-ten-six—

"Nurse," he said, "it's an appendix!"

Everybody had to cry—
not a single eye was dry.

Madeline was in his arm
in a blanket safe and warm.

In a car with a red light
they drove out into the night.

Madeline woke up two hours
later, in a room with flowers.

Madeline soon ate and drank.

On her bed there was a crank,

and a crack on the ceiling had the habit
of sometimes looking like a rabbit.

Outside were birds, trees, and sky—

and so ten days passed quickly by.

One nice morning Miss Clavel said,

"Isn't this a fine—

day to visit

Madeline."

VISITORS FROM TWO TO FOUR

read a sign outside her door.

Tiptoeing with solemn face,

with some flowers and a vase,

in they walked and then said, "Ahhh,"
when they saw the toys and candy
and the dollhouse from Papa.

But the biggest surprise by far—

on her stomach

was a scar!

"Good-bye," they said, "we'll come again,"

and the little girls left in the rain.

They went home and broke their bread

brushed their teeth

and went to bed.

In the middle of the night
Miss Clavel turned on the light
and said, "Something is not right!"

And afraid of a disaster

Miss Clavel ran fast

and faster,

and she said, "Please children do —
tell me what is troubling you?"

And all the little girls cried, “Boohoo,

we want to have our appendix out, too!”

"Good night, little girls!
Thank the Lord you are well!
And now go to sleep!"
said Miss Clavel.

And she turned out the light—
and closed the door—
and that's all there is—
there isn't any more.